My dear Rose,

It's been only a few days since we left, but my heart is heavy at the thought of being so far from you. And it seems that this voyage has only just begun.

Good news: we've finally picked up the path of the Snake by following the trail of vanishing planets. Fox and I have decided to visit all the worlds that are about to disappear into darkness, to intervene before the Snake can inject his venom there. The first planet that we've found is a hostile land, scoured by violent winds. Is this the work of the Snake?

Knowing that you're reading these words fills me with courage. Don't worry. All will be well…

The Little Prince

First American edition published in 2012 by Graphic Universe™.

Le Petit Prince ™

based on the masterpiece by Antoine de Saint-Exupéry

© 2012 LPPM
An animated series based on the novel *Le Petit Prince* by Antoine de Saint-Exupéry
Developed for television by Matthieu Delaporte, Alexandre de la Patellière, and Bertrand Gatignol
Directed by Pierre-Alain Chartier

© 2012 ÉDITIONS GLÉNAT
Copyright © 2012 by Lerner Publishing Group, Inc., for the current edition

Graphic Universe™
A division of Lerner Publishing Group, Inc.
241 First Avenue North
Minneapolis, MN 55401 U.S.A.

Website address: www.lernerbooks.com

Library of Congress Cataloging-in-Publication Data

Dorison, Guillaume.
　　[Planète des Éoliens. English]
　　The Planet of Wind / by Delphine Dubos ; adapted by Guillaume Dorison ; based on the masterpiece by Antoine de Saint-Exupéry ; illustrated by Élyum Studio, Diane Fayolle, and Jérôme Benoit ; translation, Carol Klio Burrell. — 1st American ed.
　　　　p. cm. — (The little prince ; #01)
　　　　ISBN 978—0—7613—8751—0 (lib. bdg. : alk. paper)
　　　　1. Graphic novels. I. Fayolle, Diane. II. Benoit, Jérôme. III. Saint-Exupéry, Antoine de, 1900—1944. Petit Prince. IV. Élyum Studio. V. Petit Prince (Television program) VI. Title.
PZ7.7.D67Pl 2012
741.5'944—dc23
　　　　　　　　　　　　　　　　　　　　　　　　　　　　　　　　　　　2011047352

Manufactured in the United States of America
1 — DP — 7/15/12

THE NEW ADVENTURES
BASED ON THE MASTERPIECE BY ANTOINE DE SAINT-EXUPÉRY

The Little Prince

THE PLANET OF WIND

Based on the animated series and an original story by Delphine Dubos

Design: Élyum Studio
Adaptation: Guillaume Dorison
Artistic Direction: Didier Poli
Art: Diane Fayolle
Backgrounds: Jérôme Benoit
Coloring: Digikore
Editing: Didier Poli
Editorial Consultant: Didier Convard

Translation: Carol Burrell
Bonus Story Translation: Anne and Owen Smith

Graphic Universe™ • Minneapolis • New York

★ THE LITTLE PRINCE

The Little Prince has extraordinary gifts. His sense of wonder allows him to discover what no one else can see. The Little Prince can communicate with all the beings in the universe, even the animals and plants. His powers grow over the course of his adventures.

The Prince's uniform:
When he wears the uniform of a prince, he is more agile and quick. When faced with difficult situations, the Little Prince also carries a sword that lets him sketch and bring to life anything from his imagination.

His sketchbook:
When he is not in his Prince's clothing, the Little Prince carries a sketchbook. When he blows on the pages, they take wing and form objects that he'll find very useful. Like his sword, it's powered by stardust collected on his travels.

★ FOX

A grouch, a trickster, and, so he says, interested only in his next meal, Fox is in reality the Little Prince's best friend. As such, he is always there to give him help, but also just as much to help him to grow and to learn about the world.

★ THE SNAKE

Even though the Little Prince still does not know exactly why, there can be no doubt that the Snake has set his mind to plunging the entire universe into darkness! And to accomplish his goal, this malicious being is ready to use any form of deception. However, the Snake never takes action himself. He prefers to bring out the wickedness in those beings he has chosen to bite, tempting them to put their own worlds in danger.

★ THE GLOOMIES

When people who have been "bitten" by the Snake have completely destroyed their own planets, they become Gloomies, slaves to their Snake master. The Gloomies act as a group and carry out the Snake's most vile orders so as to get the better of the Little Prince!

FATHER, THE WINDS ARE TOO STRONG. WE HAVE TO GO BACK!

NO! WE'RE ALMOST THERE! WE CAN REACH THE GREAT WIND OF LEGEND! WE JUST NEED MORE MUSIC!

IT'S NOT WORKING. WE'RE GOING TO CRASH!

I'M SORRY, EOLUS. YOU'LL HAVE TO FIND THE LEGENDARY WIND ON YOUR OWN...

NO, WAIT! THERE'S ANOTHER WAY OUT!

FIFTY YEARS LATER...

YEEEHAAH!

HA HA HA!

OUCH!

WHOOF! DO YOU THINK HE'S REALLY INTERESTED IN AN ICE PLANET, LITTLE PRINCE?

WITHOUT A DOUBT, FOX. THIS STAR SYSTEM IS ON THE WAY TO DESTRUCTION. THE SNAKE IS HERE, AND WE HAVE TO STOP HIM!

LOOK AT THOSE CREATURES...

...THEY USE AIR CURRENTS TO MELT THE ICE.

WE'RE ACTUALLY ON A PLANET OF WINDS!

BRAVO. WHAT GREAT DETECTIVE WORK!

LISTEN. IT SOUNDS LIKE A DISTANT MELODY...

THE WIND IS DROPPING!

OH! LOOK THERE...

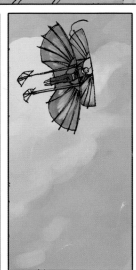

HURRY! WE HAVE TO HELP!

THAT'S FOR SURE!

7

WHAT ARE YOU DOING HERE? GO AWAY, BEFORE YOU GET TRAPPED BY THE ICE!

WE CAN'T LEAVE YOU LIKE THIS. ANYWAY, WE'RE IN NO DANGER HERE...

UH... MAYBE WE SHOULD LISTEN TO HIM.

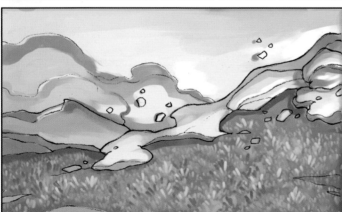

PEOPLE CALL ME THE LITTLE PRINCE, AND THEY OFTEN SAY THAT I'M VERY STUBBORN!

UM... CLEARLY.

THANK YOU. MY NAME IS FOEHN.

MR. FOEHN, DO YOU KNOW IF IT'S THE SNAKE WHO'S CAUSING TROUBLE HERE?

THE WHAT? LATER, LITTLE PRINCE. TELL ME LATER.

WE NEED TO GET BACK TO THE CITY BEFORE WE'RE SWALLOWED BY THE AVALANCHE.

IS YOUR SECRET HIDEOUT STILL FAR AWAY?

HIDEOUT? DON'T YOU KNOW? THE CITY OF WINDS IS ONE OF THE RARE SHELTERS WHERE THE WIND CURRENTS STILL SUSTAIN THE EOLUX.

THE EOLUX? ARE THOSE THE FLYING CREATURES THAT MAKE HEAT?

YES. WITHOUT THEM, OUR PLANET WOULD FREEZE OVER!

IS THAT WHY, WHEN THE WIND DROPS, THERE'S NOTHING TO STOP THE ICE?

EXACTLY!

JUMP!

OOF. THAT WAS CLOSE.

MY REAR END IS COLD.

I'LL PRESENT YOU TO THE GOVERNOR OF THE WINDS. IF YOU HAVE INFORMATION ABOUT THE WIND PIRATES, HE'LL REWARD YOU.

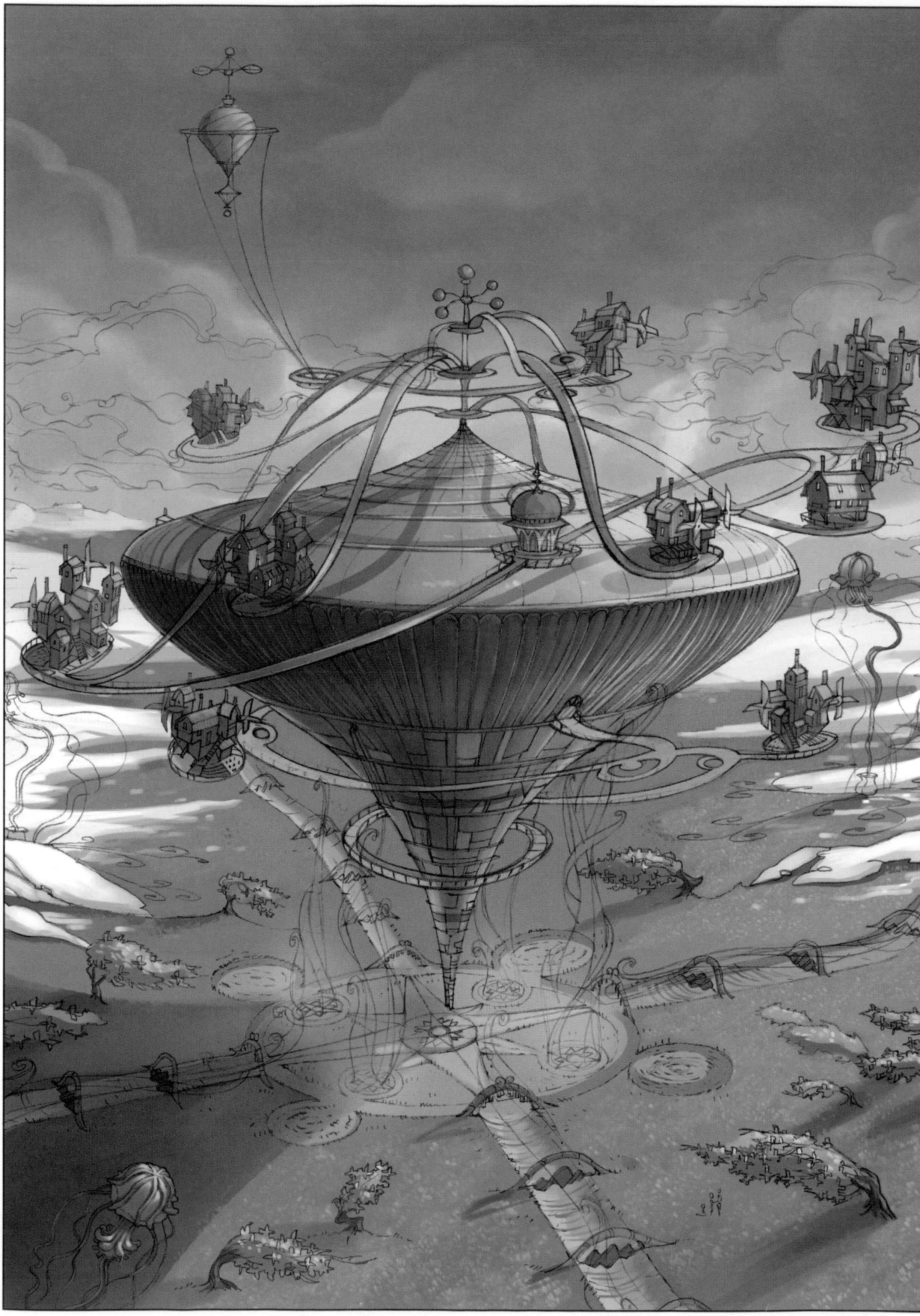

AND YOU HAVEN'T SEEN ANYTHING YET! THE AIR CURRENTS ARE DRAWN IN HERE AND RISE UP TO THE HALL OF WINDS, WHERE THEY ARE TRANSFORMED INTO WATER, HEAT, AND LIGHT...

YOUR VILLAGE IS TRULY MARVELOUS!

...WE USE THESE WIND LIFTS TO GET TO OUR HOUSES AND THE PALACE.

ACTUALLY, THE ICE WASN'T SO BAD...

WHOA!

IT ALL SEEMS SO PEACEFUL HERE. WHAT WERE YOU DOING IN SUCH A DANGEROUS PLACE, MR. FOEHN?

THE GOVERNOR OF THE WINDS, EOLUS, ORDERED ME TO FIND THE WIND PIRATES. WE DON'T KNOW HOW OR WHY, BUT THEY STEAL THE WINDS WITH THEIR MUSIC!

AT LEAST I'M NOT COMING BACK EMPTY-HANDED, THANKS TO YOU.

WE'D BE GLAD TO HELP YOUR GOVERNOR, BUT WE DON'T KNOW ANYTHING ABOUT PIRATES, JUST THE SNAKE...

AT LEAST IT'S A START, LITTLE PRINCE. ALL OUR TECHNOLOGY IS BASED ON WIND. WITHOUT IT, THIS CITY COULD NO LONGER STAY IN THE AIR. WE HAVE TO DO SOMETHING.

IT'S NOT SO BAD HERE. CAN I GO HUNTING?

SERGEANT FOEHN, BACK FROM A MISSION WITH VITAL INFORMATION FOR EOLUS. I REQUEST AN IMMEDIATE AUDIENCE!

WHAT HELD YOU UP, FOEHN?

I HAD AN ACCIDENT WITH MY MONOCOPTER DURING MY PATROL, GRANDMASTER. THE LITTLE PRINCE AND FOX HELPED ME.

THANK YOU FOR YOUR HELP, LITTLE PRINCE. BUT YOU'RE NOT FROM HERE...WHY HAVE YOU COME?

FOX AND I ARE TRAVELING THE UNIVERSE ON THE TRAIL OF THE SNAKE. HE'S AN EVIL BEING WHO DESTROYS PLANETS.

A SNAKE?

FOEHN, WHAT DOES THIS MEAN? YOU DISTURBED ME FOR THIS NONSENSE?

YES, GRANDMASTER EOLUS. WE KNOW NOTHING ABOUT THESE WIND THIEVES...MAYBE THIS SNAKE CAN LEAD US TO THEM!

HMM. INDEED, ANY BIT OF INFORMATION THAT ALLOWS US TO GET THE BETTER OF THESE VULTURES IS USEFUL.

HA HA HA!

YOU'LL HAVE TO COME UP WITH SOMETHING BETTER, FATHER, IF YOU DON'T WANT PEOPLE TO FIND THE SKELETONS IN YOUR CLOSET.

PLEASE PARDON MY SON ZEPHYR. WE WERE JUST DISCUSSING HIS FUTURE WHEN YOU ARRIVED.

EVEN THOUGH OUR WORLD IS IN DANGER AND HE IS MY HEIR, ZEPHYR REFUSES TO APPLY HIMSELF TO HIS STUDY OF THE WINDS!

SORRY IF I'M NOT JUST LIKE YOU, BUT I HAVE THE RIGHT TO CHOOSE A MORE EXCITING LIFE!

GUARDS!

ESCORT MY SON TO HIS CHAMBERS AND DON'T LET HIM LEAVE FOR ANY REASON. HE HAS STUDYING TO DO!

GOOD LUCK WITH MY FATHER. HE'S SO CHARMING.

TALK ABOUT ATTITUDE!

PLEASE EXCUSE THIS INCIDENT, LITTLE PRINCE. WHAT DO YOU SAY TO VISITING THE WIND CONTROL CENTER AND TELLING ME A LITTLE MORE ABOUT YOUR... SNAKE?

HERE YOU ARE, IN THE HEART OF THE PALACE. BEHOLD THE FAMOUS WIND MACHINE, BUILT BY MY LATE LAMENTED FATHER!

THANKS TO IT, WE CAN SEE EVERYTHING ABOUT THE WINDS: THEIR SPEED, THEIR TEMPERATURE...

AND WHAT'S THIS? IT'S BEAUTIFUL!

THOSE ARE THE FEATHER ANEMOMETERS. THEY MEASURE THE LEVEL OF THE WINDS THROUGHOUT THE COUNTRYSIDE OF EOLUX, THE FROZEN PLAIN, THE CITY OF THE WINDS...

TELL US, GRANDMASTER... WITH A MACHINE LIKE THIS, WHY CAN'T YOU KEEP THE WINDS FROM FAILING?

UH...THAT IS TO SAY...IT'S A VERY COMPLEX SCIENCE. IT WOULD TAKE TOO LONG TO EXPLAIN.

PLEASE DO, MASTER EOLUS. WE HAVE PLENTY OF TIME.

UM...THE PIRATES USE MUSICAL WIND INSTRUMENTS THAT SWALLOW UP THE AIR CURRENTS TO WORK. I AM POWERLESS AGAINST THEM...

YES, BUT... WHY? WHAT DO THESE BANDITS REALLY WANT? WHY WOULD THEY ATTACK THEIR OWN PLANET?

SEE HERE, YOU CAN'T TALK TO THE GOVERNOR OF THE WINDS LIKE THAT. HE'S ALREADY DONE SO MUCH FOR US...

LET IT BE, FOEHN. HE SPEAKS THE TRUTH.

I DON'T KNOW WHO THESE PIRATES ARE OR WHY THEY'RE STEALING OUR AIR CURRENTS. PLEASE, LITTLE PRINCE, TELL ME MORE ABOUT THE SNAKE.

HE'S A WICKED BEING WHO PROWLS THE PLANETS TO CORRUPT THEIR INHABITANTS, BY BRINGING OUT THEIR DARKEST THOUGHTS...

...AND SO THE SNAKE NEVER WORKS ALONE. IF YOUR PIRATES ARE UNDER HIS INFLUENCE, WE MUST HELP THEM SHAKE HIM OFF--NOT NECESSARILY BY FIGHTING.

FINE. IN THAT CASE, FOEHN CAN SHOW YOU AROUND OUR CITY, SO YOU CAN SEE FOR YOURSELF!

HA...THAT'S A GOOD IDEA! WE CAN FINALLY GET SOMETHING TO EAT!

THANK YOU FOR YOUR CONFIDENCE, MASTER EOLUS. WE'LL GET ON IT RIGHT AWAY.

COULD WE START BY SEEING ZEPHYR? HIS BEHAVIOR IS VERY INTRIGUING.

IMPOSSIBLE. HE'S CONFINED TO HIS CHAMBERS TO STUDY. HE CAN'T LEAVE OR BE DISTURBED.

DRAT. THEN LET'S INVESTIGATE THE CITY AS PLANNED!

WHO WAS THAT?

THAT WAS THE CAPTAIN OF THE GOVERNOR'S PERSONAL GUARD. HE'S ALSO IN CHARGE OF THE PROTECTION OF THE CITY. HE IS ABOVE ALL SUSPICION!

YOU SUMMONED ME, SIR?

YES, CAPTAIN. I'M AFRAID THAT THE PEOPLE ARE GOING TO START ASKING QUESTIONS ABOUT THE EXISTENCE OF THE PIRATES, ESPECIALLY WITH THESE STRANGERS DIGGING INTO OUR AFFAIRS.

I'M COUNTING ON YOU TO HANDLE THIS. MAKE SURE THOSE FANTASIES TAKE ON A LITTLE MORE LIFE!

WE CAN'T GO ON LIKE THIS! WE'VE ALREADY LOST MOST OF OUR FARMLAND BECAUSE OF THIS HORRIBLE ICE. AT THIS RATE, THE CITY WILL DIE.

HAVE YOU SEEN THE PIRATES WITH YOUR OWN EYES?

WHAT ARE YOU SUGGESTING, LITTLE BOY? LIKE EVERYONE ELSE HERE, I'VE HEARD THEIR MUSIC THAT STEALS OUR WINDS. THAT'S PROOF ENOUGH, RIGHT?

CALM DOWN, SIR.

WARNING! WARNING!

A PIRATE!

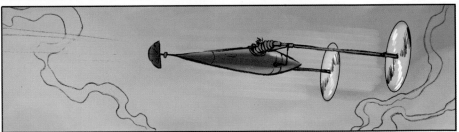

PERFECT. NOW WE CAN GET TO THE BOTTOM OF THIS.

COME ON! THERE'S NO TIME TO LOSE!

ISN'T THIS DANGEROUS? THE CURRENT COULD FAIL IF YOU STEAL TOO CLOSE TO HIM.

DON'T WORRY. HE NEEDS AS MUCH AIR AS WE DO TO STAY ALOFT.

ALL RIGHT. YOU'RE VERY CLEVER, LITTLE PRINCE.

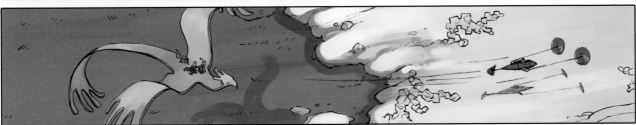

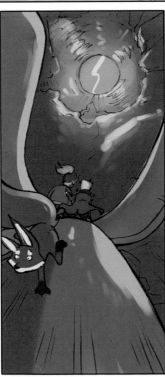

WE...WE CAN'T GO ANY FARTHER. HE'S HEADED FOR THE FROZEN PLAIN. NO ONE'S EVER COME BACK FROM THERE!

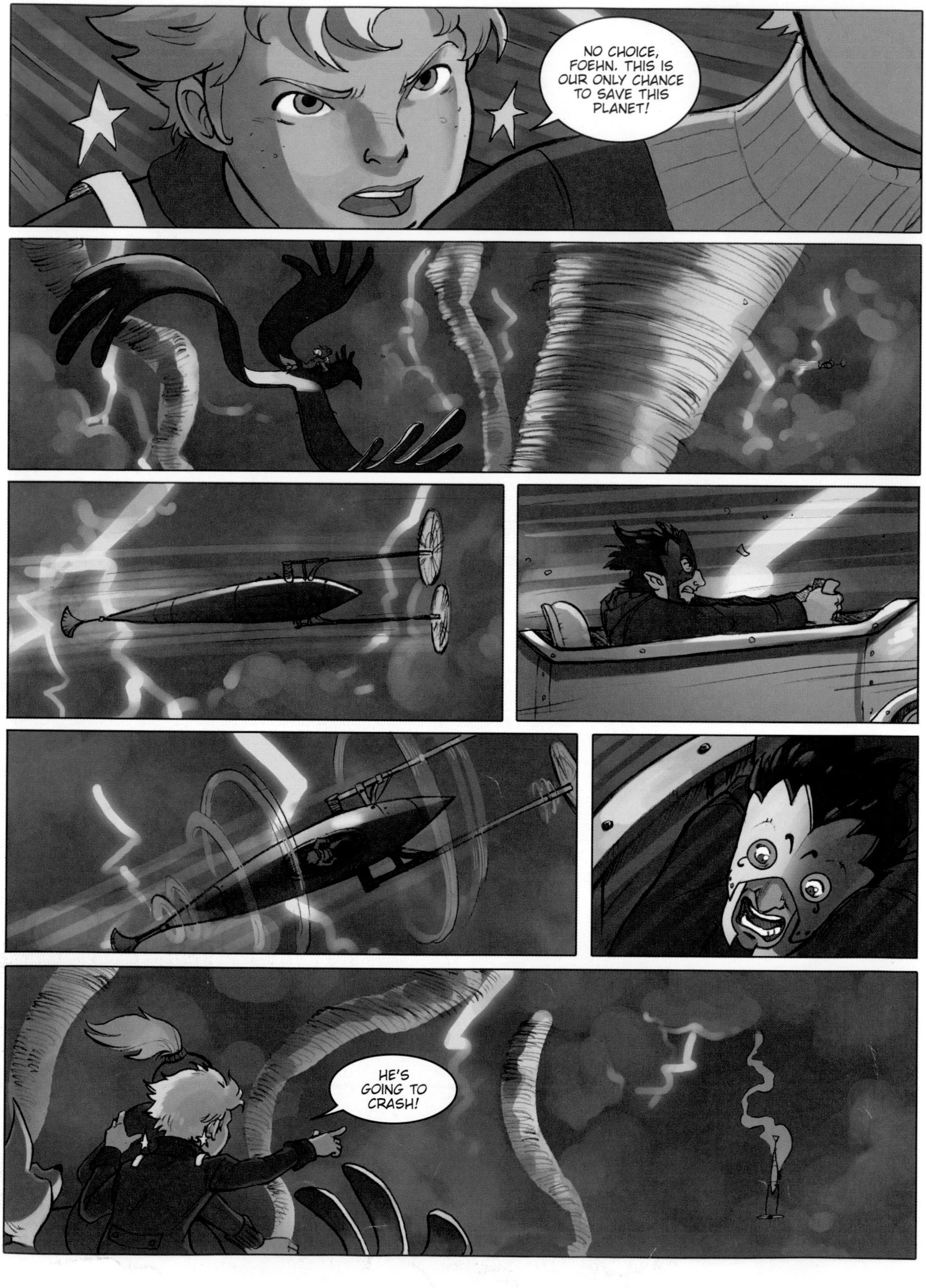
NO CHOICE, FOEHN. THIS IS OUR ONLY CHANCE TO SAVE THIS PLANET!
HE'S GOING TO CRASH!

OOF... WE'RE HAVING MORE LUCK THAN HE DID!

CAN WE TURN BACK NOW?

NOT UNTIL WE HELP THE PIRATE, FOX.

NO. WE HAVE TO GET OUT OF HERE BEFORE WE MEET THE SAME FATE. DON'T WORRY ABOUT HIM. HE'LL FIND A WAY OUT, WITH HIS WIND VESSEL. HE'S BETTER OFF, IN ANY CASE, THAN YOUR FURRY FRIEND, WHO ISN'T USED TO THIS CLIMATE.

BUT... BUT WE CAN'T LEAVE HIM LIKE THAT... I CAN'T...

LITTLE PRINCE, WE'LL ALL BE KILLED IF WE GO ON LIKE THIS. THE SNAKE WILL WIN AND THE WHOLE UNIVERSE WILL BE IN DANGER. YOU HAVE RESPONSIBILITIES!

VERY WELL. LET'S GO BACK. I HAVE TO TAKE CARE OF YOU FIRST...

FEAR NOT, MY FRIENDS! WE'VE CHASED THE PIRATES INTO THE FROZEN PLAIN!

THE WIND WILL NEVER FAIL AGAIN! WE'RE SAVED!

HEY... WHAT'S WRONG WITH THE LITTLE PRINCE?

HE BLAMES HIMSELF... THE PRINCE THINKS HE CAN SAVE EVERYONE, EVERY TIME. SO, HE'S EVEN WORRIED ABOUT THAT PIRATE.

TELL ME, FOX. HOW COME NO ONE'S SEEN THESE PIRATES UP CLOSE? AND WHY WASN'T THERE ANY MUSIC WHEN THEY ATTACKED TODAY?

WE NEED TO TALK TO EOLUS!

YOU WERE SUPPOSED TO BRING THE PIRATES TO LIFE, NOT MAKE THEM DISAPPEAR...

...CAPTAIN.

IT WAS THE STRANGERS. THEY CHASED ME! TO AVOID GETTING CAUGHT AND REVEALING YOUR PLAN, I HAD TO FLY NEAR THE FROZEN PLAIN...I ALMOST GOT KILLED!

BUT NOW EVERYONE THINKS THE PROBLEM IS SOLVED!

WHAT WILL I TELL THEM WHEN MY SON PLAYS HIS WIND ORGAN AGAIN? WOULD YOU HAVE ME DENOUNCE MY OWN FAMILY?

MAYBE IF YOU AGREE TO TELL ZEPHYR WHERE THE GREAT WIND OF LEGEND IS, HIS MUSIC WON'T BE A PROBLEM ANYMORE.

DO YOU THINK SO? ABOVE ALL, I MUST THINK OF THE FUTURE OF THIS PLANET...

HSSS... YOU CANNOT DO THAT, GRANDMASTER... WHO WOULD TAKE OVER AFTER YOU? YOUR SON MUST STUDY. HSSS...

BUT...I CAN'T SHUT HIM IN HIS ROOM FOREVER, AND I CERTAINLY CAN'T TELL THE PEOPLE THE TRUTH.

BUT NEITHER CAN YOU GIVE HIM WHAT HE WANTS. IF YOU TELL HIM THE LOCATION OF THE GREAT WIND OF LEGEND, HE'LL BE DOOMED TO CERTAIN DEATH. HSSS...

...WHILE YOU'RE WAITING FOR ZEPHYR TO SEE REASON, YOU CAN FIND A NEW SCAPEGOAT!

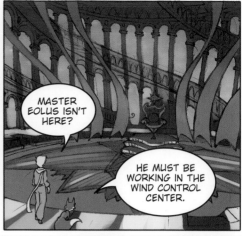

MASTER EOLUS ISN'T HERE?

HE MUST BE WORKING IN THE WIND CONTROL CENTER.

SOMETHING'S WRONG. THERE ISN'T A SINGLE GUARD. WE SHOULD BE EXTRA CAREFUL...

DON'T BE SCARED. I KNOW WHAT I'M DOING. THERE'S NOTHING TO BE AFRAID OF HERE.

MAYBE YOU WERE RIGHT, FOX.

THE GOVERNOR OF THE WINDS WOULD NEVER LEAVE HIS MACHINE UNATTENDED. MAYBE SOMETHING HAPPENED TO HIM...

THAT'LL TEACH YOU TO BLOW ME OFF!

THE MACHINE ISN'T WORKING. THE WINDS HAVE TOTALLY STOPPED.

WE'VE CAUGHT YOU AT LAST... PIRATES!

YOU ARE UNDER ARREST, FOR TAMPERING WITH THE WIND MACHINE!

THESE ARE THE THIEVES, WHO PRETENDED TO WANT TO HELP US, ALL THE BETTER TO DECEIVE US!

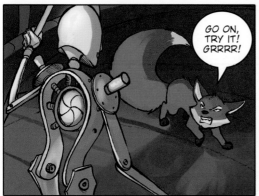

GO ON, TRY IT! GRRRR!

FOEHN! TELL THEM IT'S A TRAP!

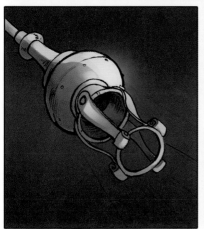

PLEASE STOP! WE DON'T WANT TO FIGHT YOU.

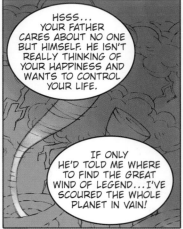

HSSS... YOUR FATHER CARES ABOUT NO ONE BUT HIMSELF. HE ISN'T REALLY THINKING OF YOUR HAPPINESS AND WANTS TO CONTROL YOUR LIFE.

HSSS...HE'LL NEVER HELP YOU... EOLUS HATES YOU BECAUSE YOU DON'T SHARE HIS PASSION FOR THE WINDS. HE'LL DO ANYTHING TO KEEP YOU FROM WHAT'S YOURS. KEEP PLAYING YOUR MUSIC, AND HE'LL EVENTUALLY GIVE IN AND TELL YOU THE LOCATION OF THE GREAT WIND OF LEGEND!

HSSS... NO ONE MUST STOP YOU FROM FULFILLING YOUR DESTINY, ZEPHYR. HSSS...

IF ONLY HE'D TOLD ME WHERE TO FIND THE GREAT WIND OF LEGEND...I'VE SCOURED THE WHOLE PLANET IN VAIN!

VERY WELL, SNAKE. I'M GOING TO SHOW MY FATHER THAT HE HAS NO CHOICE!

ZEPHYR?

DID MY FATHER SEND YOU TO SPY ON ME? TATTLETALE!

NO, NO! NOT AT ALL! I WANT TO FREE YOU. THE LITTLE PRINCE AND FOX HAVE BEEN ARRESTED. YOU HAVE TO CONVINCE THE GOVERNOR OF THE WINDS THAT THEY AREN'T OUR ENEMIES.

HA HA HA! NO KIDDING? HE'S THE ONE WHO CREATED THE PIRATE MYTH. HE'LL NEVER FREE YOUR FRIENDS!

HAVEN'T YOU EVER ASKED YOURSELF WHY NO ONE'S EVER SEEN THESE WIND THIEVES?

THERE'S STILL TIME, FOEHN. I CAN FREE THEM. HELP ME GET OUT OF HERE AND WE'LL MAKE EOLUS SORRY FOR HIS LIES!

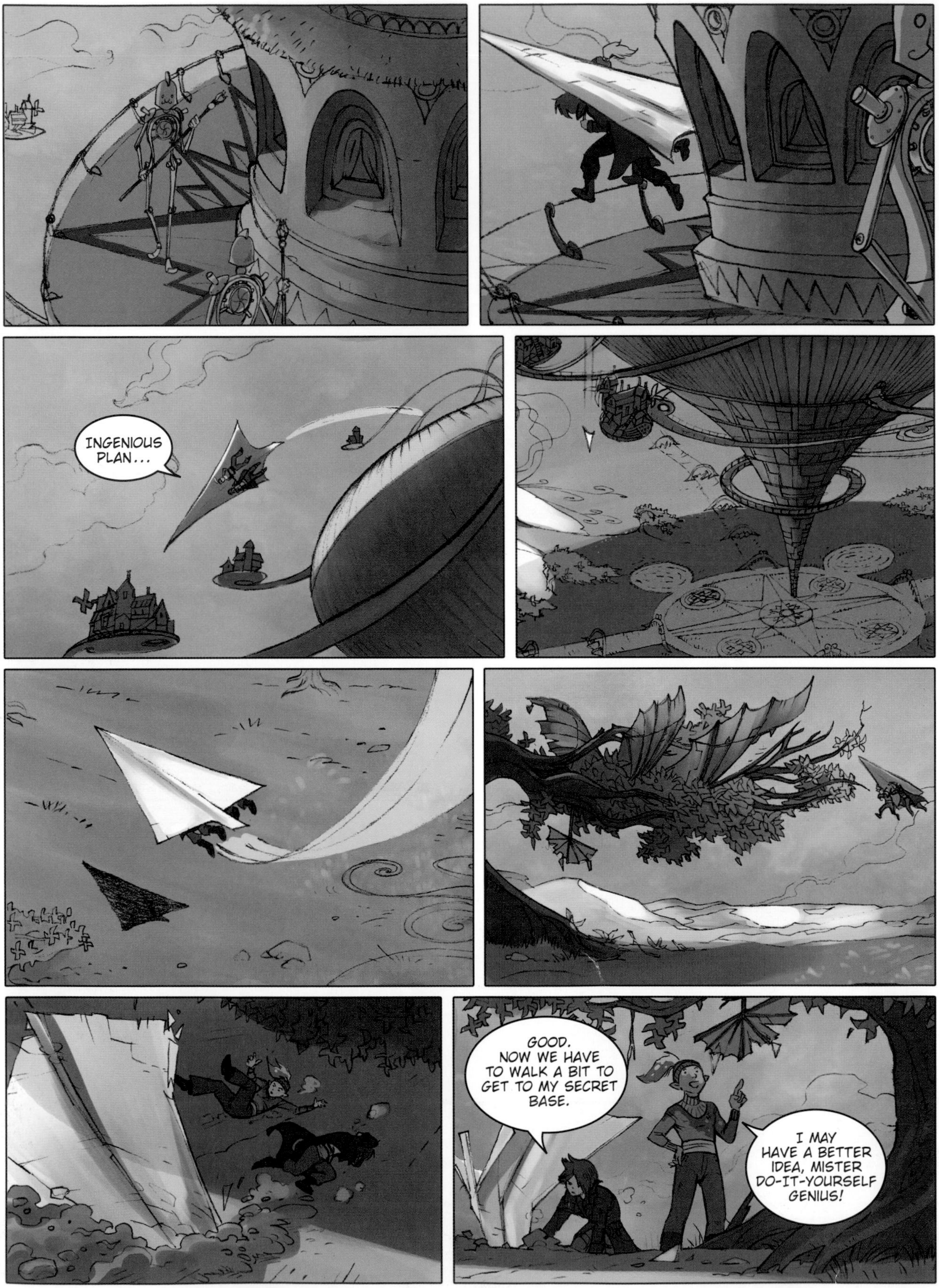
INGENIOUS PLAN...
GOOD. NOW WE HAVE TO WALK A BIT TO GET TO MY SECRET BASE.
I MAY HAVE A BETTER IDEA, MISTER DO-IT-YOURSELF GENIUS!

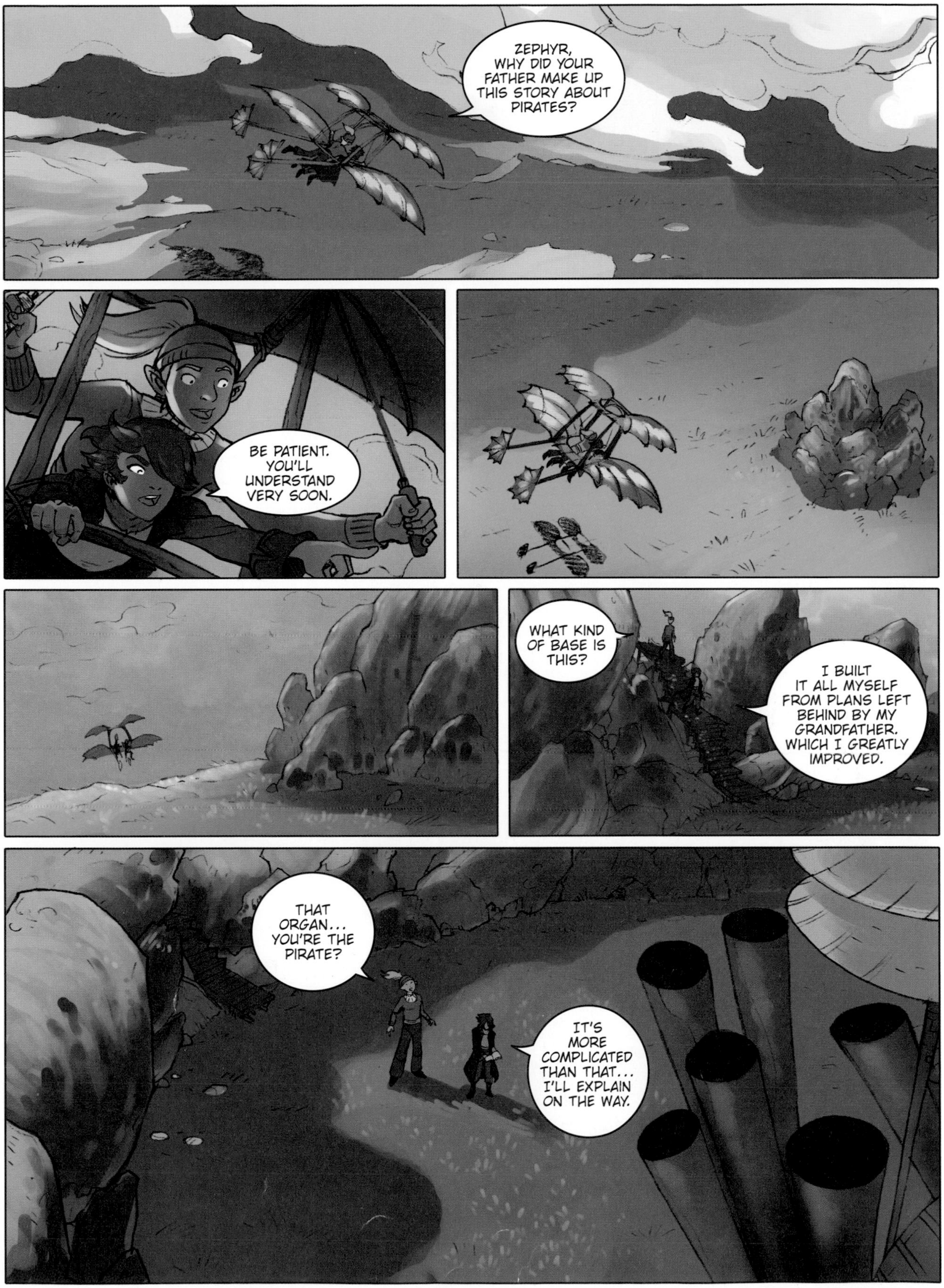
ZEPHYR, WHY DID YOUR FATHER MAKE UP THIS STORY ABOUT PIRATES?
BE PATIENT. YOU'LL UNDERSTAND VERY SOON.
WHAT KIND OF BASE IS THIS?
I BUILT IT ALL MYSELF FROM PLANS LEFT BEHIND BY MY GRANDFATHER. WHICH I GREATLY IMPROVED.
THAT ORGAN... YOU'RE THE PIRATE?
IT'S MORE COMPLICATED THAN THAT... I'LL EXPLAIN ON THE WAY.

I SHOULD HAVE GUESSED THAT MASTER EOLUS WAS BEHIND ALL OF THIS...

...AND THE SNAKE CAN'T BE FAR AWAY, EITHER.

STOP BROODING, LITTLE PRINCE. USE YOUR POWERS TO FREE US, AND WE'LL GO GIVE HIM WHAT FOR!

I CAN'T. I ALREADY USED UP LOTS OF STARDUST CHASING THE PIRATE...

...EVEN IF WE GET OUT OF THIS ROOM, WE'LL STILL HAVE TO DEAL WITH THE GUARDS AND THE HEIGHT!

I'M SORRY, FOX. WE'RE NOT GOING TO GET FED...JUST FED UP. HA HA!

AS IF EATING IS ALL I CARE ABOUT.

BUT... HEY...DID YOU JUST MAKE A JOKE? THE SITUATION IS AS HOPELESS AS THAT?

MAKE FUN IF YOU WANT...I WAS JUST TRYING TO BE LIKE YOU AND PUT THINGS IN PERSPECTIVE.

LISTEN! IT'S THE MELODY THAT WE HEARD WHEN FOEHN'S AIRCRAFT CRASHED!

IT'S THEM! THE REAL PIRATES! THE WIND IS GOING TO FALL BECAUSE OF THEIR MUSIC, AND US WITH IT!

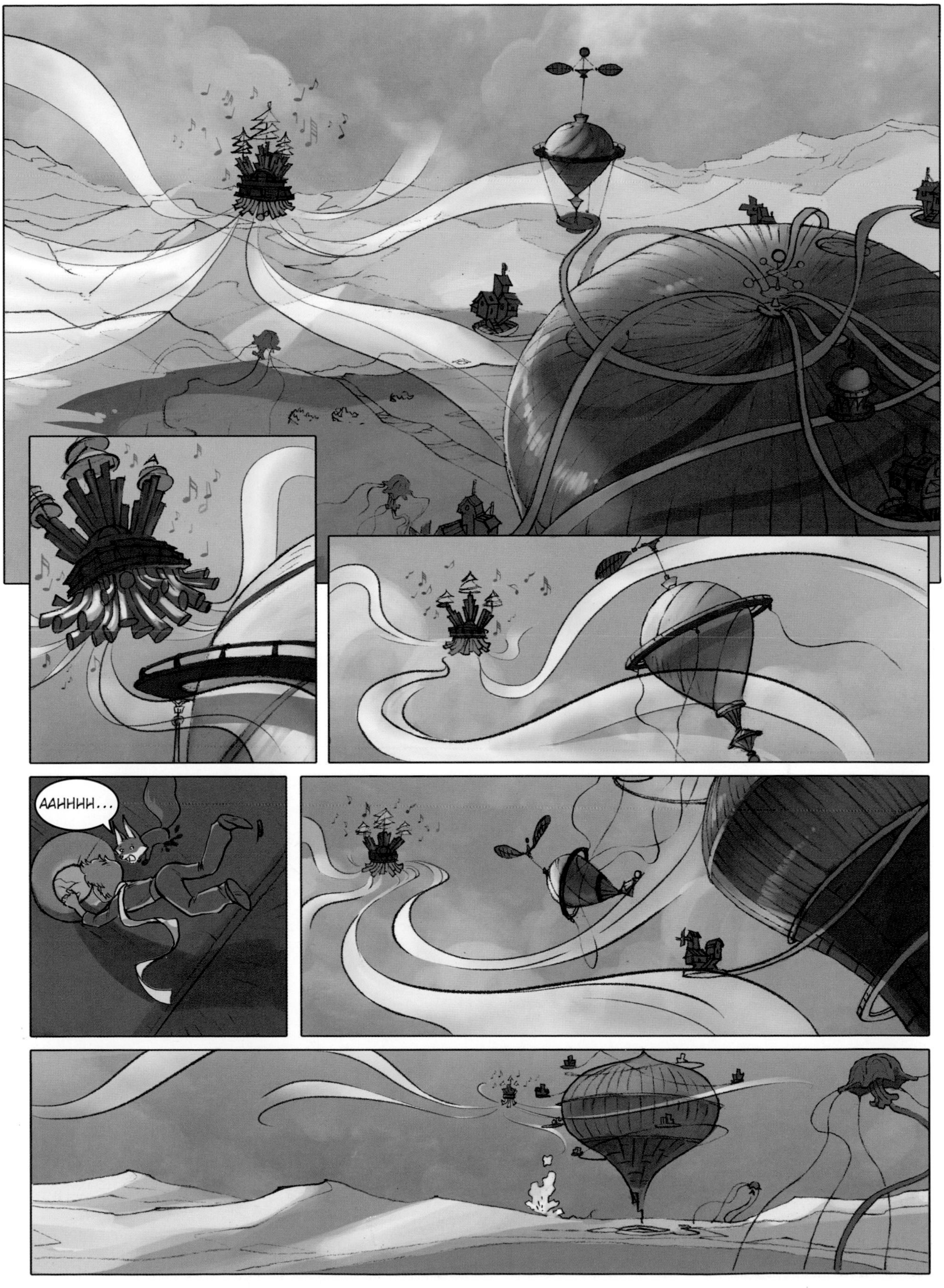
AAHHHH...

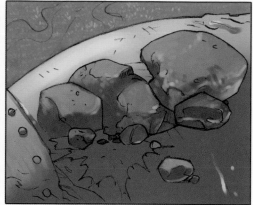

OOF...

GRRR... WICKED PIRATES, THEY NEARLY KILLED US! IF I GET MY PAWS ON THEM...

THINK ABOUT IT, FOX--THAT WAS THE ONLY WAY FOR THEM TO FREE US.

LOOK! THEY'VE ALSO GOTTEN RID OF THE GUARDS.

BAH. WELL, TELL THEM THERE ARE STILL SOME LEFT!

WAIT, WHAT... FOEHN?!

GO! I'LL KEEP THEM BUSY.

ME TOO! I WANT SOME FUN...

THE PIRATES ARE WAITING FOR US. COME ON.

YOU'RE ABANDONING YOUR FRIENDS, NOW?

NO, I'M LEARNING TO TRUST THEM.

THIS IS OUR ONLY CHANCE TO UNDERSTAND WHAT'S HAPPENING HERE!

HANG IN THERE, FOEHN! WE'LL BE BACK SOON!

WITHOUT A DOUBT, IT'S THIS MACHINE THAT'S ABSORBING THE AIR CURRENTS!

DO YOU THINK THE PIRATES HAVE CAPTURED US TO EAT US?!

IT'S NOT LIKELY THEY WANT TO HURT US, OR FOEHN WOULD NEVER HAVE JOINED WITH THEM...

YOU'RE VERY SHREWD, LITTLE PRINCE.

THINK I EVEN KNOW WHO IT IS...

WELCOME TO MY FLYING INSTRUMENT!

YOUR MUSIC IS GORGEOUS. BUT WHY ARE YOU USING IT TO STEAL THE WINDS?

WHAAAT? ZEPHYR IS THE PIRATE? HE'S THE ONE WHO GOT US INTO THIS WHOLE MESS?

SO I AM, LITTLE PRINCE. THE FALL OF THE WINDS, THE ADVANCE OF THE ICE...MY MUSIC CAUSED ALL THESE DISASTERS.

BUT IF YOU KNOW THAT, WHY CONTINUE? HOW COULD YOU LET MASTER EOLUS COVER UP YOUR WRONGDOING AND BLAME US IN YOUR PLACE?

MY FATHER?

IT'S ALL HIS FAULT! HE WON'T DO WHAT HAS TO BE DONE TO SAVE THIS PLANET!

MY MUSIC ISN'T INCOMPATIBLE WITH THE WIND CURRENTS. IN FACT, IT'S THE SOLUTION TO ALL OUR PROBLEMS.

THIS IS MY GRANDFATHER'S LOGBOOK, WHICH DESCRIBES HIS VOYAGE TO FIND THE GREAT WIND OF LEGEND: A WIND THAT CAN SUSTAIN THE EOLUX FOREVER.

THE GREAT WIND IS PROTECTED BY A ZONE OF EXTREME TURBULENCE. IN ORDER TO CROSS THAT ZONE, MY GRANDFATHER DESIGNED A FLYING ORGAN THAT USES MUSIC TO CONTROL THE STRENGTH OF THE WINDS!

UNFORTUNATELY, HIS MUSIC WASN'T STRONG ENOUGH, AND HE PERISHED BEFORE HE COULD WRITE DOWN THE EXACT LOCATION.

EOLUS, WHO WAS WITH HIM, IS THE ONLY ONE WHO KNOWS WHERE TO FIND IT.

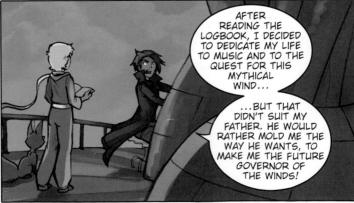

AFTER READING THE LOGBOOK, I DECIDED TO DEDICATE MY LIFE TO MUSIC AND TO THE QUEST FOR THIS MYTHICAL WIND...

...BUT THAT DIDN'T SUIT MY FATHER. HE WOULD RATHER MOLD ME THE WAY HE WANTS, TO MAKE ME THE FUTURE GOVERNOR OF THE WINDS!

HMM...YOU'RE JUST STEALING THE WINDS TO FORCE MASTER EOLUS TO TELL YOU WHERE TO FIND THIS WIND OF LEGEND!

IS THAT WHY YOU RESCUED US? SO YOUR FATHER HAS NO OTHER CHOICE BUT TO GIVE IN TO YOUR BLACKMAIL?

I UNDERSTAND HOW YOU FEEL. I ALWAYS WANT TO HELP OTHERS TOO. BUT SOMETIMES YOU HAVE TO COMPROMISE, EVEN WHEN YOU'RE RIGHT.

HSSS... THINK ABOUT WHAT YOU DESIRE, ZEPHYR. EOLUS WILL BE VERY JEALOUS WHEN YOU DISCOVER THE GREAT WIND OF LEGEND AND BECOME A HERO. HSSS...

HSSS... DON'T LET THESE STRANGERS TURN YOU FROM YOUR TRUE MISSION!

LET'S GO TALK TO THE GOVERNOR OF THE WINDS. I'M SURE THAT, TOGETHER, WE'LL FIND A WAY TO SOLVE YOUR PROBLEMS WITHOUT PUTTING THE PLANET IN DANGER!

YOU'RE TOO NAIVE, LITTLE PRINCE! THERE'S ONLY ONE WAY TO BREAK MY FATHER'S OPPOSITION!

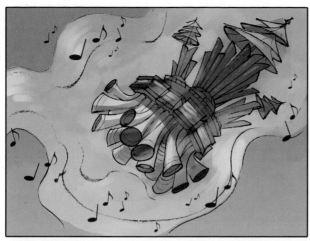

LITTLE PRINCE! HELP!

NOOO!

GNIIIIII...

THAT WAS CLOSE!

HERE THEY COME. THEY DIDN'T WASTE ANY TIME.

IT'S GOOD TO BE BACK ON SOLID GROUND.

HMPH. YOU HAVE A LOT OF NERVE COMING BACK HERE, AFTER DESTROYING THE PRISON AND HELPING THAT TRAITOR FOEHN RUN AWAY!

SEE! HE GOT AWAY.

MASTER EOLUS, GIVE US A CHANCE TO EXPLAIN BEFORE YOU PUNISH US.

AND WHY SHOULD I?

OH, WE JUST WANT TO TALK ABOUT ZEPHYR AND YOUR LITTLE SECRET...

YOU SEEM TO KNOW ALL ABOUT IT ALREADY, LITTLE PRINCE, SO YOU UNDERSTAND WHY MY SON MUST ABSOLUTELY STOP PLAYING HIS MUSIC!

I DO UNDERSTAND, MASTER EOLUS. BUT WHY REFUSE TO LET HIM REALIZE HIS DREAM?

ZEPHYR IS YOUNG AND IDEALISTIC. CHASING AFTER THE GREAT WIND OF LEGEND WON'T TEACH HIM HOW TO RULE THE CITY WHEN I'M NO LONGER HERE!

WHY SHOULD DEFENDING THIS PLANET BE THE JOB OF YOUR FAMILY ALONE? SHARE THIS RESPONSIBILITY WITH OTHERS AND LET YOUR SON FOLLOW HIS OWN PATH!

AND GIVE IN TO HIS BLACKMAIL?

WHY DON'T YOU TELL US THE REAL REASON WHY YOU REFUSE TO TALK ABOUT THE WIND OF LEGEND?

YOU ARE WILIER THAN I THOUGHT, FOX...

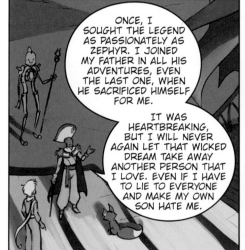

ONCE, I SOUGHT THE LEGEND AS PASSIONATELY AS ZEPHYR. I JOINED MY FATHER IN ALL HIS ADVENTURES, EVEN THE LAST ONE, WHEN HE SACRIFICED HIMSELF FOR ME.

IT WAS HEARTBREAKING, BUT I WILL NEVER AGAIN LET THAT WICKED DREAM TAKE AWAY ANOTHER PERSON THAT I LOVE. EVEN IF I HAVE TO LIE TO EVERYONE AND MAKE MY OWN SON HATE ME.

HAVE YOU EVER OPENED YOUR FEELINGS LIKE THIS TO YOUR SON?

MASTER! A CATASTROPHE!

THE ICE HAS REACHED THE CITY, AND THE PEOPLE ARE STORMING THE PALACE GATES!

LET US SEE EOLUS! THESE LIES MUST STOP!

SORRY, FOEHN. I DON'T KNOW WHERE THOSE WICKED PIRATES ARE...

WE MUST EVACUATE THE CITY BEFORE THE ICE OVERWHELMS US.

LIAR! FOEHN TOLD US EVERYTHING! IT'S YOUR SON'S FAULT! DO YOUR DUTY!

GRANDMASTER, I UNDERSTAND YOUR SORROW, AND ZEPHYR'S, BUT IT'S GONE TOO FAR! YOU CAN'T CONDEMN US ALL IN HIS PLACE!

LOCK ME UP, PUNISH ME...BUT DON'T ASK ME TO MAKE MY OWN CHILD A CRIMINAL. HE'S ALL I HAVE LEFT!

IT'S NEVER TOO LATE, FATHER!

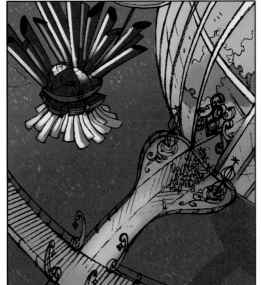

EOLIANS! PEOPLE OF THE PLANET OF THE WIND! YOU HAVE BEEN MISLED, BUT I CAN SAVE YOU. THANKS TO MY MUSIC, I'M CLOSE TO GETTING MY HANDS ON THE GREAT WIND OF LEGEND!

MAKE THE GOVERNOR OF THE WINDS REVEAL TO ME WHERE TO FIND IT, AND I'LL FLY OFF AND STEAL IT FOR YOU. YOU WILL BE RID OF THE ICE FOREVER!

OUT OF THE QUESTION!

I BEG YOU, TELL HIM WHAT HE WANTS TO KNOW. IT'S OUR ONLY CHANCE!

LOOK OUT! NOOOOOO!

SHOW YOURSELF, SNAKE! I KNOW THAT YOU'RE BEHIND ALL OF THIS!

HSSS... YESSS...AND I HAVE WON. ZEPHYR WILL NEVER FORGIVE HIMSELF FOR HIS FATHER'S DEATH, AND THIS STAR SYSTEM WILL BE DESTROYED. HSSS...

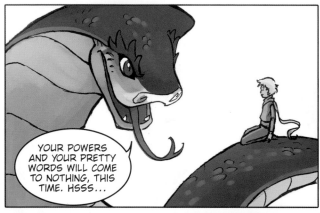

YOUR POWERS AND YOUR PRETTY WORDS WILL COME TO NOTHING, THIS TIME. HSSS...

ON THE OTHER HAND, I CAN STILL HELP YOU.

ANOTHER TEMPTATION, SNAKE? YOU'LL NEVER GET ANYTHING FROM ME!

HSSS... I EXPECT NOTHING IN RETURN, LITTLE PRINCE. I WAS JUST GOING TO TELL YOU WHERE TO LOOK FOR THE GREAT WIND OF LEGEND. GO FIND IT AND SAVE THE PLANET OF WIND!

I'LL TAKE YOUR ADVICE, SNAKE.

LITTLE PRINCE! LITTLE PRINCE, WAKE UP!

IT'S ALL RIGHT! ZEPHYR USED HIS FLYING MACHINE TO CATCH HIS FATHER BEFORE HE HIT THE GROUND.

I... I'M GOING TO STOP BEING SO SELFISH AND FORGET ABOUT THIS STUPID QUEST.

S-SORRY TO HAVE SHATTERED ALL YOUR DREAMS, ZEPHYR. I ONLY WANTED TO PROTECT YOU...

DON'T BLAME YOUSELVES TOO MUCH. YOUR ACTIONS WERE INFLUENCED BY THE SNAKE!

BECAUSE YOU WOULDN'T TALK TO EACH OTHER, HE TOOK ADVANTAGE OF IT TO SET YOU AGAINST EACH OTHER AND SEND YOUR WORLD INTO PERIL.

MASTER EOLUS, YOU LIED FOR ZEPHYR AT THE RISK OF LOSING EVERYTHING YOU'VE WORKED FOR ALL THESE YEARS...

...AND ZEPHYR, TO PROTECT YOUR PEOPLE, YOU TOOK ON YOUR OWN SHOULDERS THE RESPONSIBILITY TO SUCCEED WHERE YOUR ANCESTORS FAILED.

THE ONLY MISTAKE YOU BOTH MADE WAS NOT SHARING YOUR FEELINGS.

EVEN IF YOU'RE RIGHT, LITTLE PRINCE, I CAN'T BRING MYSELF TO TELL YOU ABOUT THE GREAT WIND OF LEGEND.

YOU WON'T HAVE TO. THANKS TO THE SNAKE, I KNOW WHERE TO GO NOW. YOU'LL BE PROUD OF YOUR SON, GRANDMASTER.

LET'S GO RIGHT AWAY. THE ICE IS AT THE GATES OF THE CITY! ZEPHYR, FOEHN, I NEED YOUR TALENTS!

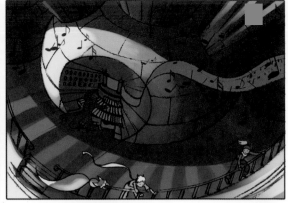

ARE YOU SURE ABOUT THIS? REMEMBER WHAT HAPPENED TO THE PIRATE THE LAST TIME!

THIS IS THE ONLY WAY TO GET TO THE GREAT WIND OF LEGEND!

THIS IS FOLLY! I'VE ALREADY SCOURED THE FROZEN PLAIN DOZENS OF TIMES. THERE'S NOTHING HERE!

LITTLE PRINCE, I'VE TRIED IN VAIN TO SHOW ZEPHYR THE BEST CURRENTS FOR NAVIGATING. WE WON'T LAST LONG AT THIS PACE.

ZEPHYR, THE LOUDER YOUR MUSIC, THE MORE THE ORGAN ABSORBS THE WINDS, MAKES THEM LESS FIERCE, RIGHT?

RIGHT, BUT I'VE REACHED MY LIMIT!

PERFECT! I HAVE A PLAN!

HEAD FOR THE TORNADO THAT'S IN FRONT OF US AND FLY INTO IT AT FULL SPEED.

WHAT?? YOU MUST BE CRAZY. IT'LL CRUSH US!

TRUST ME. NOTHING IS IMPOSSIBLE IF WE WORK TOGETHER.

HURRY! IT'S OUR LAST CHANCE. EVERYONE IS COUNTING ON US!

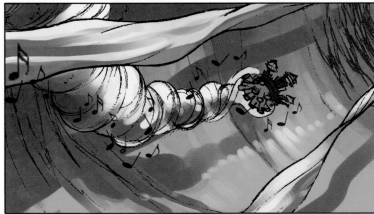

WITH THIS, WE SHOULD BE ABLE TO AMPLIFY YOUR MUSIC AND HAVE THE POWER THAT YOUR GRANDFATHER DIDN'T.

WE DID IT! WE FOUND THE GREAT WIND OF LEGEND!

UM, SORRY TO PUT A CHILL ON THE MOOD, BUT WHERE IS THIS SUPER-WIND? 'CAUSE I DON'T FEEL ANYTHING.

THAT'S TRUE... THERE ISN'T EVEN A BREEZE.

THE GREAT WIND OF LEGEND IS MAGICAL AND IMPERCEPTIBLE.

IN FACT, ONLY THE WIND MACHINE CAN DETECT ITS PRESENCE AND USE IT!

BUT THEN... HOW DO WE COLLECT IT? WE CAN'T MOVE THE WIND CONTROL CENTER HERE!

CALM DOWN, FOEHN. ZEPHYR'S GRANDFATHER MUST HAVE PLANNED FOR THAT WHEN HE DESIGNED THE ORGAN.

IN FACT, I'M SURE HE BASED IT ON THE SAME MECHANISM AS THE WIND MACHINE IN THE PALACE!

OF COURSE! THAT'S WHY YOU HAD ME COME ALONG!

YES, BY COMBINING YOUR KNOWLEDGE OF THE WINDS WITH ZEPHYR'S MUSIC, WE'LL BE ABLE TO BRING THE GREAT WIND OF LEGEND BACK TO THE CITY.

UH...WHAT DO YOU MEAN BY ALL THAT, ROUGHLY SPEAKING?

THAT WE'RE GOING TO ZEPHYR'S FIRST BIG CONCERT!

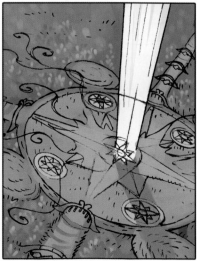

IT'S A MIRACLE! THE ICE IS MELTING!

THANK YOU, LITTLE PRINCE AND FOX, FOR BELIEVING IN ME.

COME BACK WHENEVER YOU WANT. WE'LL GO FLY KITES.

SURE... AND I HOPE WE'LL GET A LESS CHILLY RECEPTION, NEXT TIME!

BY THE WAY... WHY DID THE SNAKE TELL YOU WHERE TO FIND THE GREAT WIND OF LEGEND? HAS HE LOST HIS MIND?

HA HA HA! NO, HE WAS TRYING ONE OF HIS MOST VILE SCHEMES. I'M SURE HE HOPED WE WOULD ALL PERISH ON THE FROZEN PLAIN TRYING TO REACH OUR GOAL...

BUT HE UNDERESTIMATED OUR FRIENDS!

THE END

The Little Prince

AS IMAGINED BY
MOEBIUS

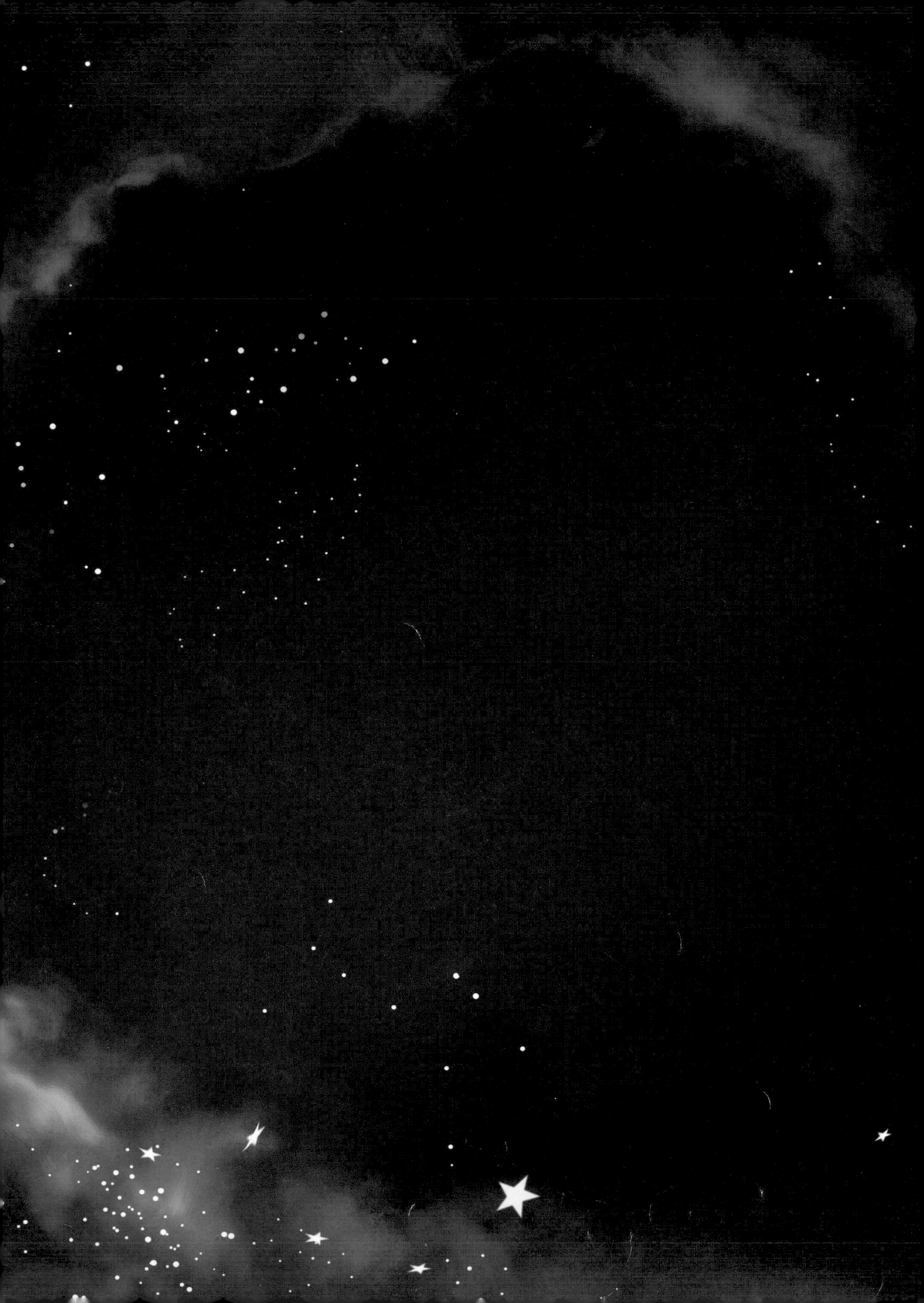

THE LITTLE PRINCE

"ON THE PLANET OF CORNERS"

THERE IT IS! THE PLANET OF CORNERS!

BUT...IT'S A CUBE! A BIG BLOCK!

UH, YEAH. IT'S A FREAK OF NATURE!

WE'RE GOING TO MAKE A LITTLE VISIT TO THE HEAD BLOCK!

OOOH, THE BLOCKHEAD... NOT BAD!!!

I'M SURE HE'S GOT A WELL-ROUNDED PERSONALITY!

HA HA HA!

DETACH THE BUBBLE AND WE'LL TAKE A CLOSER LOOK, LITTLE FOX!

LITTLE? ME?

GOOD NEWS: THE AIR IS BREATHABLE...

THAT'S LUCKY! I LIKE BREATHING!

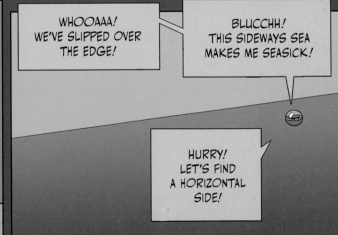

WHOOAAA! WE'VE SLIPPED OVER THE EDGE!

BLUCCHH! THIS SIDEWAYS SEA MAKES ME SEASICK!

HURRY! LET'S FIND A HORIZONTAL SIDE!

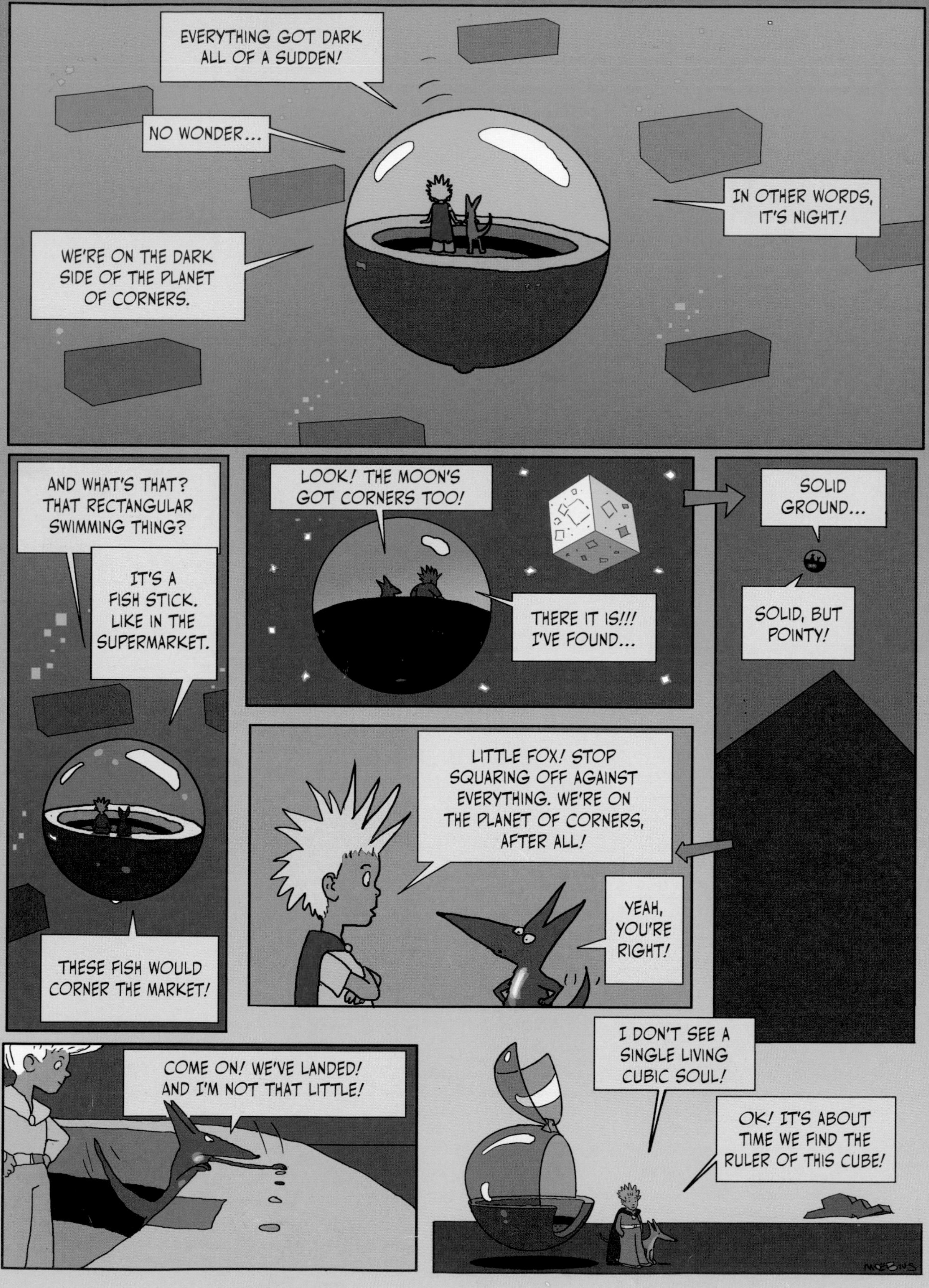
EVERYTHING GOT DARK ALL OF A SUDDEN!
NO WONDER...
WE'RE ON THE DARK SIDE OF THE PLANET OF CORNERS.
IN OTHER WORDS, IT'S NIGHT!
AND WHAT'S THAT? THAT RECTANGULAR SWIMMING THING?
IT'S A FISH STICK. LIKE IN THE SUPERMARKET.
THESE FISH WOULD CORNER THE MARKET!
LOOK! THE MOON'S GOT CORNERS TOO!
THERE IT IS!!! I'VE FOUND...
SOLID GROUND...
SOLID, BUT POINTY!
LITTLE FOX! STOP SQUARING OFF AGAINST EVERYTHING. WE'RE ON THE PLANET OF CORNERS, AFTER ALL!
YEAH, YOU'RE RIGHT!
COME ON! WE'VE LANDED! AND I'M NOT THAT LITTLE!
I DON'T SEE A SINGLE LIVING CUBIC SOUL!
OK! IT'S ABOUT TIME WE FIND THE RULER OF THIS CUBE!
MOEBIUS

LET'S WALK OVER TO A SUNNY SIDE. THAT WOULD MAKE IT EASIER TO SEARCH!
HEY! AREN'T YOU HOT AT 90 DEGREES?
AT LEAST IT'S DAYTIME HERE!
OVER THERE! I SEE SOMETHING...
THE RULER!
APPROACH!
STATE YOUR IDENTITY, PLEASE.
NAME, ADDRESS, TELEPHONE NUMBER...
I'M THE LITTLE PRINCE BY ANTOINE DE SAINT-EXUPÉRY. MY FRIEND IS THE LITTLE FOX.
HEY! FOX FOR SHORT!
AND I'M ANTI-TELEPHONE. IT KEEPS PEOPLE APART!
THAT'S NEVER BEEN SCIENTIFICALLY PROVEN!
NOT TO MENTION ALL THAT ELECTRO-MAGNETIC POLLUTION!
THAT'S A MATTER OF OPINION.
HMPH! SOUNDS LIKE CIRCULAR REASONING TO ME...
HOW DREADFUL!
ANYWAY...WHILE WE'RE ON THE SUBJECT...
I'D LIKE TO SEE YOUR TRAVEL PERMIT.
I HAVE A SPECIAL "LITTLE PRINCE" PASS.
IN THAT CASE, LET'S HAVE A SPOT OF TEA.
?
THE S.L.P.P. GIVES YOU THE RIGHT TO ONE CUP OF TEA. THEN YOU MUST CROSS BACK.
SOUNDS LIKE A SQUARE DEAL.
I'LL GIVE YOU A PASSPORT SIGNED BY MY OWN HAND.
IT SEEMS LIKE HE WAS SAD TO SEE US LEAVE. HIS RIGID RULES MAKE HIM A RUEFUL RULER!
HE'S PAINTED HIMSELF INTO A CORNER!
BIG FOX! I DON'T BELIEVE IT! LOOK AT HOW THE RULER SIGNED THE PASSPORT!
OF COURSE! IT SAYS: PAUL E. GONE, THE RULER OF CUBE-A...

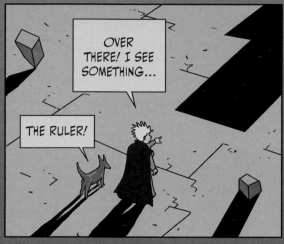

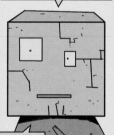

ANTOINE DE SAINT-EXUPÉRY
Aviator • Author • Adventurer • Hero

Antoine de Saint-Exupéry, author of the novel *The Little Prince* on which these new adventures are based, was born on June 29, 1900, in Lyon, France. He was the third of five children: Marie-Madeleine, Simone, Antoine, François, and Gabrielle. It was when he was twelve years old, during his summer break from boarding school, that airplanes and flying first made a huge impression on him.

In 1920, he was accepted into the École des Beaux-Arts in Paris to study architecture, but the next year he joined the Second Aviation Regiment of the armed forces and received his pilot's license. In 1922, he had his first plane crash, and suffered a head fracture. He had to leave the armed forces and work at different jobs on the ground to earn a living.

By May of 1926, Saint-Exupéry was able to fly again. He delivered airmail, which was a new and sometimes dangerous profession, on routes from France to Senegal and all the way to South America. That was where, in 1931, he met and married Consuelo Suncin.

From 1933 to 1938, Saint-Exupéry was very busy. He traveled to North Africa and Indochina, and attempted to break the flight speed record from Paris to Saigon, Vietnam—during which his plane crashed again. It went down in the middle of the Sahara Desert. After his recovery, his life became even busier. He wrote newspaper reports in Spain on the Spanish Civil War, scouted airplane routes between Casablanca and Timbuktu, wrote a screenplay, registered several patents, and traveled to the United States. In 1939, with the start of World War II, he returned to France and talked his way into a job as a high-risk reconnaissance pilot for the French Air Force. But this only lasted until France reached an armistice agreement with Germany.

In December 1940, Saint-Exupéry returned to visit friends in New York, where he finally began work on *The Little Prince*. The story is narrated by a pilot who has crashed his plane into the Sahara Desert. He meets a little prince visiting from a faraway asteroid. Along the way, the prince also meets Fox and Snake. By late 1942, after spending the spring and summer writing and illustrating, Saint-Exupéry had completed his novel, and in April 1943 it was published in his native language of French (*Le Petit Prince*) and in English.

Saint-Exupéry was eager to return to the war. He decided to join the Free French Forces in Algeria, who were continuing the fight against the Axis powers. Because of his age, at first he had a hard time convincing them to let him fly. He was authorized to fly five dangerous missions. In fact, he flew eight. On July 31, 1944, Saint-Exupéry went on a scouting flight to prepare for military landings in the south of France. His plane disappeared over the water, and he was never seen again.

Over the decades since *The Little Prince* was published, it has gone on to become one of the best-selling novels of all time. In 2003, a small moon in our solar system's asteroid belt was named Petit-Prince in honor of the masterpiece Saint-Exupéry created.

After several years in video games and Japanese animation, adapter Guillaume Dorison became literary editor for the publisher Les Humanoïdes Associés in 2006, where he launched the Shogun Collection dedicated to original manga. In June 2010, he founded Élyum Studio with Didier Poli, Jean-Baptiste Hostache, and Xavier Dorison to provide services for the creation of graphic novels. In addition to his position as director of writing for Élyum Studio, he has more than two dozen comics and manga to his credit under the pseudonym IZU, has written several titles in the Explora series on world explorers for French publisher Glénat, and won the 2010 Animeland Prize for best French manga.

Didier Poli, artistic director for the new graphic novel adaptations based on The Little Prince, was born in Lyon in 1971. After graduate studies in applied arts, he worked for various animation studios including Disney. He was working as artistic director for the video game company Kalisto Entertainment when he met Manuel Bichebois in 2001 and began drawing Bichebois' graphic novel series L'Enfant de l'orage. At the 2004 Nîmes Festival, Didier Poli received the Bronze Boar prize for young talent. He continues, along with his work on graphic novels, to work regularly in cartoons and video games as a designer and storyboard artist.